Lucky's Choice

SUSAN JESCHKE

SCHOLASTIC
HARDCOVER

SCHOLASTIC INC., New York

Library of Congress Cataloging-in-Publication Data
Jeschke, Susan.
Lucky's Choice.
Summary: Lucky, a comfortable but unloved cat,
risks his home when he refuses to kill a mouse he
has befriended.
[1. Cats—Fiction.   2. Mice—Fiction]   I. Title.
PZ7.J553Lu 1987   [E]   86-2075
ISBN 0-590-40520-9

12 11 10 9 8 7 6 5 4 3 2 1   7 8 9/8 0 1 2/9
Printed in the U.S.A.   10
First Scholastic printing, March 1987

For Roger

Lucky was a house cat
who lived in a very clean, locked apartment.
Each day his owner fed him, then left for work.
He passed the day eating and sleeping and watching TV.

He watched *Jungle Cat*, which was about a clever tiger...

...and *Wes and the Witch* (his favorite).

Wes was a witch's cat. The witch adored Wes and took him everywhere.

The high point of Lucky's day was watching for the Cat Lady, who came to visit the alley cats each afternoon.

Lucky wished he could get out so that he, too, could be petted and loved. But the window wouldn't budge.

His owner was always telling him how *lucky* he was that he *wasn't* an alley cat. That's why he thought Lucky was his name.

When his owner came home, Lucky greeted her warmly.
He hoped she would pick him up and cuddle him.
But she didn't.

She fed him, saying either "good kitty" or "*bad* kitty"
(depending on the damage she found),
and the usual "aren't you lucky to be housed, fed,
and not have a worry in the world —
unlike those miserable alley cats."

One night, Lucky tried to snuggle up to her in bed.
"Bad kitty — off the quilt!" she said...

...and promptly put him out of the room.
"Go sleep in your own bed," she said.

Lucky went to bed and dreamed he was Wes, the witch's cat
— flying on her broom, being held in her arms,
and sitting by her cozy fire.

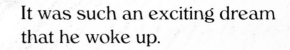

It was such an exciting dream
that he woke up.

He longed to tell his dream to someone,
but the bedroom door was locked...

...and the alley was deserted.

"Never mind," he thought. He jumped on the table
and began telling his dream to a pretend audience.
He acted everything out.
"Quiet out there!" his owner shouted.

Lucky paused. He saw something move.

A mouse! The first real mouse
that Lucky had ever seen!

He lunged and caught it.
"Uh...wait! That was a...a...
great dream," the mouse said

...and fainted away.

Lucky was stunned and very flattered.
He worked frantically to revive
the mouse.

That was how Lucky met Ezra.

When he grew tired of waiting,
he would just reach into the hole
and drag Ezra out.

From then on Lucky waited
for Ezra to come out of his hole
behind the stove.

As the days went by, Ezra began to see that
he was wanted as a playmate, not as a snack,
and they became friends.

Lucky thought that Ezra was very clever and wise.

Ezra told Lucky that the reason he had dreamed of being the witch's cat was because he wanted to have adventure and love, just like Wes.
"But you got safety. You can't have everything. You got it good here," Ezra said.

Maybe Ezra was right, Lucky thought.

Although he didn't have a witch to love him,
he had Ezra, and that made the days pass happily.

One day, after playing very hard, Lucky and Ezra fell asleep
and didn't hear the click of the key in the lock.

He ran off and hid.
She followed him.
"Why do you think you're here?"
she shouted. "I want that mouse dead!"

"A mouse!" shrieked Lucky's owner
as Ezra scurried off. "KILL IT!"

The words sent shivers through Lucky.

Every evening, she would ask,
"Have you killed it?"
Lucky pretended he didn't understand.

"You silly, worthless cat! You don't know how
lucky you are that I keep you," she said.

Lucky did know that he couldn't kill
his best and only friend.

His owner cut back on
his food to make him hungrier.

She threatened to get an exterminator,
or another cat, and she began laying
poison traps.

Lucky was very worried for Ezra
and carefully removed all the poisoned cheese
and pretended to play with it.
When his owner saw that, she made a final threat.

"If I don't see a dead mouse in this house in 24 hours, you're *out*!"

Out? Out where? Lucky wondered. He asked Ezra.
"She means out there, pal," Ezra said,
pointing to the alley. "Out there it's a real jungle.
Not like on TV. You'd be lost."

Now it was Ezra who was worried.
He decided to leave.
"All I've ever wanted is to be a house mouse,"
he said. "This was the best place ever,
and you're the best friend ever. You got it good here,
and I'm not going to ruin it for you. Good-bye."

Ezra leaped toward the windowsill — but
Lucky stopped him and held him fast.

"Put me down or eat me up!" Ezra demanded.

Lucky's mind was racing.

All he could think of
was what his life was like
before Ezra.

Suddenly he knew
what to do.

"I'm going with you, Ezra!"

They wasted no time in working at the window screen.

Soon they were out and...

...into the alley.

They searched the garbage cans for food.

The other cats were more successful.
Lucky felt scared. He was beginning to think
he had made a mistake.

It grew chilly and the other cats disappeared.
But Lucky and Ezra had nowhere to go.

Suddenly there was the sound of footsteps coming closer.
They stopped in front of him.
Lucky felt himself being stroked...

...and lifted up.

It was the Cat Lady!
"What a wonderful, special pair you are!"
she said, noticing Ezra.

Lucky was purring so loudly that he hardly heard her say,
"I'm taking you home with me!"